# The Little Cow in Valle Grande

# El Becerrito en Valle Grande

# The LITTLE COW in VALLE GRANDE

## El Becerrito en Valle Grande

story by SKILLMAN "KIM" HUNTER

illustrations by MARY SUNDSTROM

Spanish translation by
SARAH PILCHER RITTHALER

UNIVERSITY OF NEW MEXICO PRESS ❦ ALBUQUERQUE

Printed in Hong Kong by Toppan Printing Company, Inc.

12  11  10  09  08  07  06      1  2  3  4  5  6  7

LIBRARY OF CONGRESS CATALOGING-IN-PUBLICATION DATA
Hunter, S. C. (Skillman Cannon), 1937–
The little cow in Valle Grande : El becerrito en Valle Grande /
Skillman Hunter ; illustrated by Mary Sundstrom ;
Spanish translation by Sarah Pilcher Ritthaler.
p. cm.
Summary: When a little cow ignores his mother's advice and climbs to
the top of a mountain, he finds himself tired, hungry, cold, and in need
of a fast way to get back to his mother in their beautiful meadow.
ISBN-13: 978-0-8263-4044-3 (CLOTH : ALK. PAPER)
ISBN-10: 0-8263-4044-X (CLOTH : ALK. PAPER)
1. Cows—Fiction.  2. Mothers and sons—Fiction.
3. Adventure and adventurers—Fiction.  4. Valles Caldera (N.M.)—Fiction.
5. Spanish  language materials—Bilingual.]  I. Sundstrom, Mary, ill.
II. Ritthaler, Sarah Pilcher.  III. Title.
PZ73.H86 2006
[E]—dc22

2006007864

Book design and composition: Kathleen Sparkes
This book typeset using Utopia 16/26
Display type is Incognito

THIS BOOK IS DEDICATED
TO MY GRANDCHILDREN:

George Hunter Bird

Cameron Russell Bird

Jacqueline Helen Hunter

Matthew Belforte Hunter

Kaitlyn Elizabeth King

*and*

Ryan Hunter King


MY FATHER,

Russell Vernon Hunter

WHO CREATED THE ORIGINAL
MANUSCRIPT IN 1941


AND MY MOTHER

Virginia McGee Ewing

WHO SAVED THE MANUSCRIPT

IN MEMORIAM

John D. Wirth

*Kim's original introduction
to this story when
he was a kid . . .*

This story was made by John
Wirth and me when John was
three and a half years old
and I was two and a half.

I lived in Santa Fe, New Mexico,
and I liked to visit my friend John at Los Alamos where
there were many boys at a school.

The place is very beautiful. It is in the high mountains
where you can ski and skate in the winter. In the summer
you can swim and go for picnics.

Nearby is a big meadow, which is called Valle Grande.
Valle Grande was a good place to picnic. We went there
one day when it was nice and warm and weathery.
In Valle Grande we saw the little cow and many other cows.

When we got back to John's house, our mothers were very
tired. They were too tired to read the stories we already
knew. So we made up this one. It was fun to make it up

that night when the big fireplace had a warm fire in it. The mountain country is very cold at night.

We have made this story over many, many times. It is fun if you say the words in red. You can change this story if you want to. You can name the little cow Charles or give him any name you like. You can have him live at Pinocchio's house (which I think is very funny) or where you live, or where you go for picnics. You can make other changes, too. One thing John and I never wanted to change was the mother cow. I will soon be four.

*Kim's comment at printing . . .*
I am so glad this turned out to be a bilingual edition. This book is dedicated to "Mamacita." My earliest memory, about age five, was walking to the house where Mamacita cooked tortillas every morning. There was always one for me and they were so delicious. *¡Muy bien gracias, Mamacita!*

$\mathcal{O}$nce upon a time there was a **little cow** and his name was **Buddie**.

$\mathcal{H}$abía una vez un **becerrito**, y él se llamaba **Buddie**.

Buddie lived in a beautiful meadow in **Valle Grande.**

Buddie **vivía** en un prado hermoso en **Valle Grande.**

One day he said to his mother, "I think I will go
to **the top of the mountain.**"

Un día dijo a su madre, "Pienso ir
**a la cumbre de la montaña.**"

His mother replied, shaking her head,
"I would not advise you to go to the **top of the mountain**.
There is no **grass to eat** at the top of the mountain."

Su madre respondió, negando con la cabeza,
"Te aconsejaría que no vayas a la **cumbre de la montaña**.
No hay **pasto que comer** en la cumbre de la montaña."

Said the little cow, "**I think I shall go anyway.**"

So he started.

Dijo el becerrito, "**Siempre pienso ir.**"

Así pues, comenzó.

**Buddie** went across the **grassy meadows** and he jumped over the **arroyos**.

**Buddie** cruzó los **prados de zacate** y brincó por los **arroyos**.

Then he began to climb the **mountainside**.

He climbed until **lunchtime**.

Entonces comenzó a subir la **ladera de la montaña**.

Subió hasta **la hora de comer**.

Then he found some **grass** and **ate it**.
Then he had a **nap**.

Entonces encontró algún **pasto**, y **lo comió**.
Después durmió la **siesta**.

After his nap **he woke up** feeling refreshed and
he climbed on toward **the top of the mountain.**

Después del sueñecito **se despertó** refrescado, y
siguió subiendo hacia **la cumbre de la montaña.**

When **Buddie** got to the **top of the mountain**
his feet were very tired. The **sun** was going down
and it was **getting dark**.

꙰

Cuando **Buddie** llegó a la **cumbre de la montaña**
estaban muy cansados los pies. El **sol** estaba bajando
y **se hacía de noche**.

So he found a **big tree** and he laid down on the
leaves that were under the **tree** and **went to sleep**.

Así pues, encontró un **árbol grande** y se recostó sobre las
**hojas** que estaban debajo del **árbol, y se durmió.**

When he woke up the ground was covered with **snow**.
He said, "Now I can never find any **grass**.
My mother **was right**."

✦

Cuando se despertó el suelo estaba cubierto de **nieve**.
Dijo, "Ahora jamás podré encontrar **pasto**.
Mi madre **tenía razón**."

He shivered. It was **very cold**. He sniffed the **cold air**
and said, "I wish I could get **home** quickly!"
He tried to think of the quickest way.

Él tiritó. Hacía **mucho frío**. Respiró el **aire frío**
y dijo, "¡Ojalá pudiera llegar a **casa** muy pronto!"
Trató de pensar en la manera más rápida de hacerlo.

He remembered seeing some **children skiing**
last winter when he was a **tiny cow**.

Se acordó de haber visto a unos **niños esquiar**
el invierno pasado cuando era un **becerro pequeñito**.

So he got **two sticks** and tied them to his **feet** with some **vines**.

Entonces consiguió **dos palos** y los ató a los **pies** con unas **enredaderas**.

And **Buddie** started down **the mountainside**.

Y **Buddie** comenzó a bajar **la ladera de la montaña**.

*Whee-e-e-e-e!*

Halfway down the mountain he saw **another cow**.
And who do you think it was? It was his **mother cow**.

A mitad de la bajada, él vio **otra vaca**.
¿Y quién crees que era? Era su **madre vaca**.

He stopped as quickly as he could and said, "Mother, I am glad to see you for **I am very hungry.**"

Se paró tan pronto que pudo y dijo, "Mamá, me alegro mucho de verte, porque **tengo mucha hambre.**"

"I thought you would be," said his **mother cow**.
"I brought you some **milk**." So he drank the milk.
Then he felt **fine**.

"Ya me lo imaginata," dijo su **madre vaca**.
"Te traje **leche**." Así pues bebió la leche.
Entonces se sentía **bien**.

And he went back to **Valle Grande** with his mother,
**where he was content to live happily ever after.**

Y volvió a **Valle Grande** con su madre,
**donde vivió feliz y contento.**

## About the Hunters and the Wirths

Virginia Hunter and Virginia Wirth were introduced by Jane (Mrs. Gustave) Baumann and became friends before John and I were born. The Hunters lived in Santa Fe, where my father, Russell Vernon Hunter, was an artist and State Director of the Federal Arts Project, WPA. The Wirths lived in Los Alamos where John's father, Cecil Wirth, was headmaster at the Los Alamos Ranch School. Both families enjoyed picnics in Valle Grande.

When World War II began, the school became the location for development of the atomic bomb.

Telling this story became a bedtime ritual for my father and me. My father wrote it down so that I would have it for my grandchildren, but he died before completing the illustrations, which is the reason for this book.

# Postscript

Valle Grande is now part of Valles Caldera National Preserve, described at www.vallescaldera.gov. The little cow, his mother cow, and all their friends are still there at various times of the year. There is a visitor center you may call to find out when the cows are there.